A/i,

MW00905107

BLUE
Banner
BIOGRAPHIES

SAM DARNOLD

Marylou Morano Kjelle

PUBLISHERS

2001 SW 31st Avenue
Hallandale, FL 33009

www.mitchelllane.com

First Edition, 2020.
Author: Marylou Morano Kjelle
Designer: Ed Morgan
Editor: Lisa Petrillo

Series: Blue Banner Biographies
Title: Sam Darnold / by Marylou Morano Kjelle

Hallandale, FL : Mitchell Lane Publishers, [2020]

Library bound ISBN: 9781680205015
eBook ISBN: 9781680205022

Contents

Jet-Propelled!

AT&T **STADIUM** in Arlington, Texas, was an exciting place to be on the night of Thursday, April 26, 2018. For the 83rd time in the history of the National Football League (NFL), team owners were selecting new players. This selection is called the NFL draft, and it takes place every year. In the sports world, a draft is a common way for a team to choose new players.

The NFL draft is also a thrilling event for football fans. On this night, 40,000 enthusiastic NFL fans were eager to learn which players their favorite teams would draft. Dressed in team jerseys and hats, and waving banners and pom-poms, the fans lucky enough to be there at AT&T Stadium cheered as each team announced its pick.

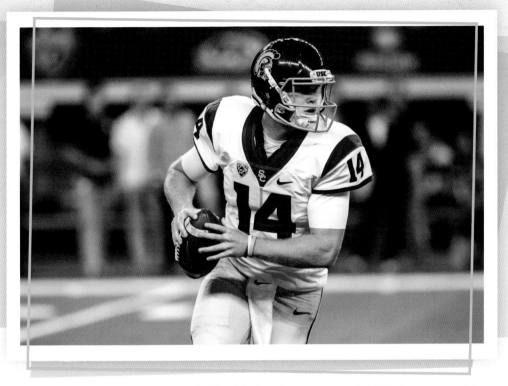

Sam Darnold planned to redshirt his freshman year at USC, but a crushing defeat at the hands of the University of Alabama's Crimson Tide on September 3, 2016, motivated him to become a full team member.

Twenty-year-old Sam Darnold was a star quarterback for the University of Southern California (USC), and he sat with his family in an off-stage area that had been set up for the draftees. The first round of the 2018 draft was about to begin. Although still in college, Darnold had officially declared himself eligible for the NFL draft a few months earlier. He explained his upcoming decision at a press conference held late in 2017. He told a reporter for the *Dayton Daily News* that the opportunity to play in the NFL was "a dream of mine."

Was tonight the night Darnold's dream of playing for the NFL would become a reality?

Darnold had broken many records as a quarterback for USC, and many sports experts had predicted that he would be the first player selected in the 2018 draft. But the team to choose first, the Cleveland Browns, selected Baker Mayfield, a quarterback from the University of Oklahoma. The second team, the New York Giants, chose Saquon Barkley, a running back from Pennsylvania State University.

Each team had 10 minutes to make its choice. The New York Jets were up next. The clock was running. The crowd roared. Darnold waited. At last, the telephone next to him jingled. It was Todd Bowles, a coach for the Jets. Coach Bowles offered Darnold a place on his team, and he accepted.

"Glad to have you, man. More than happy. It's [going to] be outstanding," said the coach. Then he put Jets' owner Chris Johnson on the line.

"I did not think that we would have a shot at you," said Johnson. "I am so happy, Dude. You are going to love New York."

"Yes, sir. It's going to be amazing. Promise you," answered Darnold. This was such a big event for the New York Jets, their interview was posted on the team website.

A few seconds later, an announcement rang out throughout the stadium.

Jet-Propelled!

"With the third pick in the 2018 NFL draft, the New York Jets select Sam Darnold, quarterback, USC."

Popping a Jets hat on his head, Darnold bounded onto the stage. There the NFL Commissioner handed him a Jets rookie jersey that had his last name and the number "1" on it, showing he was the Jets' first pick of that year's draft.

"Whatever the coaches want me to do, I'm going to star in my role," said Darnold in an interview with sports reporter Suzy Kolber later that evening.

The NFL had a new star. And this star was jet-propelled!

Darnold accepts the Jets team jersey as No. 1 draft pick from NFL Commissioner Roger Goodell on April 26, 2018.

Sports in His DNA

SAMUEL RICHARD DARNOLD was born June 4, 1997, in Capistrano Beach, California. Sam, as his family calls him, and his family love sports. His mother, Chris, is a middle school physical education teacher who in her youth played volleyball at Long Beach Community College. His father, Michael, is a medical gas plumber who works in hospitals.

Sam's father, Mike Darnold, attended one of Sam's first games as a NY Jet on September 16, 2018. The game was against the Miami Dolphins and played at MetLife Stadium in East Rutherford, New Jersey.

Mike played football in college as an offensive lineman for the Bulldogs at the University of Redlands in Redlands, California. Sam's older sister, Franki, played for the University of Rhode Island volleyball team. Three of Sam's cousins also played volleyball in high school. And Sam's grandfather, Dick Hammer, played basketball at USC—an athlete so talented he was a member of the 1964 U.S. Olympic volleyball team. (Dick was also an actor who made TV commercials.) With so many family members involved in athletics, you could say that Sam has sports in his DNA!

When he was a toddler, Sam didn't talk much, but he sure was active. He was so energetic that his parents had to withdraw him from his first day care for being too lively. Sam started swimming lessons when he was three years old, and Taekwondo karate classes when he was four. Sam's parents thought these activities would help him use up some of his extra energy. By the time he was five, Sam was playing basketball in his backyard with his dog, Libby. He also played soccer and baseball.

As for football, Sam has loved it ever since he saw his first game on television. When he was in elementary school, Sam and his father played football in their backyard every chance they got.

"[Football is] something I was born to do," he told an interviewer on Foxsports.com.

Many parents encourage their children to focus on a single sport. Sam's parents were different. "He was so naturally gifted, it was crazy," his mother told a reporter for *Bleacher Report*. "We wanted him to be a kid and try it all. What else is a childhood for? You need to discover yourself."

Sports in His DNA

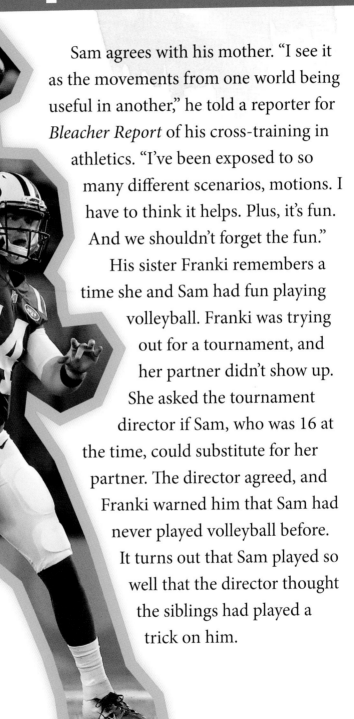

Sam agrees with his mother. "I see it as the movements from one world being useful in another," he told a reporter for *Bleacher Report* of his cross-training in athletics. "I've been exposed to so many different scenarios, motions. I have to think it helps. Plus, it's fun. And we shouldn't forget the fun."

His sister Franki remembers a time she and Sam had fun playing volleyball. Franki was trying out for a tournament, and her partner didn't show up. She asked the tournament director if Sam, who was 16 at the time, could substitute for her partner. The director agreed, and Franki warned him that Sam had never played volleyball before. It turns out that Sam played so well that the director thought the siblings had played a trick on him.

Before Sam starred on the football team at San Clemente High, he played on the school basketball team with teammates (*left to right*), Cole Fothringham, Nick Crankshaw, Elijah Morris, Cade Griffin, and Sam (*far right*).

When Sam got to San Clemente High School, he continued playing a variety of sports. As a freshman, he played baseball. In his sophomore year, he switched to basketball. His eye was good, and his arm was strong. Sometimes he sank the ball into the basket from 25 feet across the court.

"Basketball was my first love," Sam told sportswriter Paolo Ugetti in *The Ringer*. "I loved it just because it was so fast. In 2015, he shared the Sea View League's Most Valuable Player award with another San Clemente basketball player.

Sports in His DNA

Sam also started playing varsity football with the San Clemente Tritons in his sophomore year of high school. At first, Sam played the linebacker and wide receiver positions. Then, when the team's starting quarterback was injured, Sam filled in. As quarterback, Sam shattered the school record for the most touchdown passes in a game. He threw five! And he did it twice in two separate games. The next year, Sam broke his foot and had to sit out the rest of the football season. By the time his foot healed, the season was over, so Sam went back to playing basketball.

Sam's skills as a quarterback were seen early in his football career at San Clemente High School.

From Triton to Trojan

JAMIE ORTIZ was Sam's high school football coach. He thought that Sam was good enough to play on a college team after he graduated high school. Usually, a high school athlete will make a videotape to send to college recruiters so that they can see him in action. But Sam's broken foot had kept him from playing football. Coach Ortiz had no video of Sam playing football to send to colleges, so, he sent them a tape of Sam playing basketball instead.

Coach Ortiz especially wanted the football coaches at USC to take a look at Sam. They liked what they saw, and USC offered Sam a scholarship to play on its famous football team, the Trojans. Other top-level colleges offered Sam scholarships like Duke University, Northwestern University, and the University of Utah. Sam chose USC for several reasons. There was tradition, for his grandfather, Dick Hammer, had attended USC. It felt more like home, since it was close to his family home in Capistrano Beach. Sam liked that he could visit and his family could catch his games in Los Angeles.

Now in college, Sam Darnold became a communications major and put on the No. 14 jersey of the USC Trojans.

A Utah State Aggies defensive lineman attempts to tackle Darnold on September 10, 2016, at the Los Angeles Coliseum. Darnold threw two touchdown passes at this game and USC won 45-7.

USC is a member of PAC-12, a conference of twelve colleges in the West. At USC, he played quarterback, one of the most important positions in football. Sometimes, a quarterback acts as the team's leader. He calls the plays when the team goes into a huddle. The quarterback is responsible for leading the team's offense.

College athletes sometimes "sit out" or delay playing with their teams for one year. This is called redshirting. The extra time allows them to develop their skills and become better at their game. An athlete who redshirts can practice with his team but can only play four games for the season. Darnold entered the 2016 season as a redshirted freshman. Then the USC Trojans lost to the University of Alabama Crimson Tide 52–6, on September 3, 2016. It was a humiliating defeat and the worst season-opening loss in the history of USC. It was enough to get Darnold off the bench and into the game.

The following week, when USC played its second game of the season against the Utah State Aggies, Darnold threw two touchdown passes. The Trojans won 45–7. But the pride of winning didn't last long. Just one week later, the Trojans lost to the Stanford University Cardinals 27–10.

Darnold recovers his end zone fumble from Marcus Williams of the Utah Utes on September 23, 2016. USC's crushing 31–27 defeat marked a turning point in his college football career.

Darnold was the starting quarterback when USC played its next game against the Utah Utes on September 23, 2016. USC was leading by 7 points when Utah scored with 17 seconds on the clock. The crushing 31–27 defeat marked a turning point for Darnold. He reached out to former USC quarterback and NFL player, Matt Leinart, for advice. "He basically said to continue being myself because, in my darkest moments, that's who everybody's [going to] see,'" Darnold told *ESPN*.

Darnold took Leinart's advice, and USC won the next nine games. The last game was the Rose Bowl. This annual post-season college football game is usually played on January 1 at the Rose Bowl Stadium in Pasadena, California, after the famous parade. Rose Bowl 2017 was a competition between USC and the Nittany Lions of Pennsylvania State University. It was Darnold's best game so far.

He set career highs for throwing for 453 yards, which resulted in five touchdowns for the Trojans. Darnold's team won the game 52–49.

Darnold's skill is not the only thing to shine through a game. His sportsmanship does as well. "[Players] like playing with him. You see an excitement and energy when he takes the field. It kind of gives a sense of confidence as an offense, when he steps unto the huddle," Trojans offensive coordinator, Tee Martin told Foxnews.com.

What makes Darnold such a great football player? Maybe it's the way he prepares for a game. He prefers practicing in the ocean. He goes into the water up to his waist and throws a football over the five-foot waves.

Some say Darnold's unique playing style contributes to his success. "Sam's out there flinging the ball around like he's back in recess at elementary school playing catch with his friends" quarterback Max Browne told Lee Jenkins in *Sports Illustrated*. Browne also went to USC, and went on to play in the NFL for the Pittsburgh Panthers.

Darnold's personal quarterback coach, Bob Bosanko agrees. He told reporter Jenkins that "Sam gets away with stuff that isn't necessarily mechanically sound. It's because he never developed all these robotic habits when he was eight, so he doesn't think too much about his arm slot and his delivery. He just anticipates where a guy will be and puts it there. That's a quality you can't teach. That's feel."

From Triton to Trojan

Maybe it's his skill, his style or a combination of both that helped him earn many awards in 2017. He won the Archie Griffin Award, given to the player who is the most valuable to his team throughout the season. No other college freshman had ever won this award before. Also in 2017, the Football Writers' Association of America named Sam to its Freshman All-America team. Despite setbacks, Darnold led USC to a championship in PAC-12. The game against Stanford was close with USC winning by just 3 points (31–28). Darnold received the team's Most Valuable Player (MVP) award after throwing 300 yards and scoring two touchdowns.

"The kid has grown up fast, on and off the field," USC receiver Darreus Rogers told a reporter. "He has become a natural leader and his instincts on the field are amazing. What more can you ask for?"

At the Pac-12 Championship game against the Stanford Cardinals on December 1, 2017, Darnold received the team's Most Valuable Player (MVP) award after throwing 300 yards and scoring two touchdowns.

Rookie Quarterback

DURING HIS TIME at USC, Darnold was the Trojans' starting quarterback for 24 games. Of those 24 games, USC won 20. His last season with USC resulted in 11 wins. It was the best season for USC since 2008. Darnold was also the first USC quarterback to throw for more than 4,000 yards. He was considered for the Heisman Trophy, one of football's most prized awards. It is given each year to a college football player for outstanding sportsmanship.

Playing for the Trojans had taught Darnold a lot about playing football. But he was ready to play on a larger football field, and that field was the NFL. Darnold thought long and hard about declaring himself available to the NFL. He had grown as a player at USC, but now it was time to move on. Early in 2018, while still in his second year of college, Darnold announced his eligibility on social media.

"After talking to my immediate family, very close friends, and many people who have helped me throughout my life, I have made the decision to declare for the 2018 NFL draft," he explained in a video posted to his Instagram account in early January.

Darnold demonstrated his skills at football for NFL scouts during USC Trojans Pro Day on March 21, 2018.

Of course, the Trojans would have liked Darnold to continue to play for them, but they understood why he wanted to leave.

"Thank you, Sam Darnold, for being the person, player and man of character that you are! You are the true example of what it means to be a Trojan!" USC coach Clay Helton wrote back to Darnold on social media.

The New York Jets haven't won a Super Bowl since 1968. Jets officials were looking for a skilled quarterback to bring new life to their team. They recognized Darnold's potential and wanted him. They had even traded up to the number 3 spot in the draft, which would give them a better chance to select Darnold. In August 2018, he signed a contract with the Jets. He would earn $30 million over four years.

The Jets coaches liked Darnold's solid build. He is 6 feet 4 inches tall and weighs 225 pounds. They liked that he can accurately throw the ball while on the move. They were also impressed with his ability to process the layout of the players on the field and make fast decisions.

Darnold hands off to Jets team member, running back Elijah McGuire, at a mandatory Jets minicamp on June 12, 2018 in Florham Park, New Jersey.

"When I watch him, I see a lot of God-given, instinctual ability that I think is rare," said former Dallas Cowboy quarterback, Tony Romo, an analyst for the television show, "NFL on CBS."

But playing for an NFL team is not the same as playing football in high school or college. Darnold still has a lot to learn. He knows it, and the Jets know it as well.

"He still has some rookie tendencies, but he's definitely more mature than a typical rookie. He's not perfect—he knows that; we all know that—but he's pretty good," Quincy Enunwa, a Jets wide-receiver told a reporter for *ESPN*.

Darnold played his first regular season game as a New York Jet on September 10, 2018, against the Detroit Lions. Of the five quarterbacks chosen in the first round of the 2018 draft, Darnold was the only one picked to be a starter for a team's opening game. He was also the youngest quarterback to start an NFL season opening game since 1970.

"We're not starting him because he's a rookie and he's not ready. We're starting him because he gives us a good chance to win the game," Coach Bowles announced to the media at a pre-game press conference.

The Jets won 48–17. Darnold also became the first Jets player to deliver multiple touchdown passes in his first career game.

Darnold throws a pass while under pressure during his first regular season game as a New York Jet against the Detroit Lions on September 10, 2018. He becomes the first Jets player to deliver multiple touchdown passes in his first career game.

CHAPTER FIVE

A Man of Few Words

SAM DARNOLD was only two years old when his grandfather, Dick Hammer, died, so he never really got to know him. But he has heard a lot about him, and in many ways, Sam reminds Chris of her father.

"[My father] never thought of himself as a big shot, and my son never has either," Sam's mother told a reporter for *ESPN*. "Sam plays football for the love of the game, not for the fame."

Darnold may be a well-known football star, but off the field, he is a man of few words. He'd rather listen to someone else talk than be the one doing the talking. He is a no-frills kind of guy with a low-key personality who celebrated being drafted by the Jets with a pizza instead of a night on the town. To relax he does yoga and meditates. He likes to listen to sports radio shows and read self-improvement books.

Darnold also has a great deal of love and respect for his parents. "I have been blessed that my life has been full of memorable moments and wonderful people. The people who have been involved in making me the man I am today have prepared me for the life and decisions that I have to make in the future," Darnold told a *Los Angeles Times* reporter when he declared for the draft.

Darnold knows that he is young and that the long career ahead will give him the chance to grow as a football player.

"There's a lot of room for growth, but I'm also very confident in my ability to go out there and play. I'm going to do what the coaches ask me to do, and I'm going to come in here and learn right away and just go about it that way," Darnold told a reporter.

Where does Sam Darnold see himself in the future? With the New York Jets, playing—and winning—the Super Bowl, of course!

The future sure looks "super" for Sam Darnold.

Timeline

1997   Born June 5

2011–2015

Attends San Clemente High School

Awarded the South Coast League Most Valuable Player award twice for basketball

Named to the all-California Interscholastic Federation team, also for basketball

2015   Graduates San Clemente High School

Begins attending USC

2016   Named starting quarterback for USC Trojans after playing three games

Leads the Trojans to nine consecutive winning games

Receives Archie Griffin Award

Named PAC Offensive Freshman of the Year

Finalist for the 2016 Manning Award, and the O'Brien Award, both awarded to the nation's top quarterback

Named to the Football Writers' Freshman All-American first team and Campus Insiders Freshman All-American second team

Wins USC's Most Inspirational Player Award, and the Bob Chandler Award, given to player with outstanding athletic ability, academic achievement, and character

2017   Leads USC to victory at Rose Bowl on January 2

Named to First Team All PAC-12

2018   Announces his eligibility for the draft on January 3, leaving USC before graduation

Drafted by the New York Jets on April 26

Plays first regular season game September 10 against the Detroit Lions

Career Stats for 2018

Passing yards	2357
Passing touchdowns	14
Interceptions thrown	15
Passer rating	72.8%

Find Out More

Books

Editors of *Sports Illustrated. 1st and 10 (Revised and Updated): Top 10 Lists of Everything in Football (Sports Illustrated Kids Top 10 Lists). Sports Illustrated Kids*, 2016.

Gramling, Gary. *The Football Fanbook: Everything You Need to Become a Gridiron Know-it-All (A Sports Illustrated Kids Book)*. Sports Illustrated Kids, 2017.

Jacobs, Gregg. *The Everything Kids' Football Book: All-time Greats, Legendary Teams, and Today's Favorite Players—with Tips on Playing Like a Pro*. Adams Media, 2016.

On the Internet

Official Website of the NY Jets
https://www.newyorkjets.com/

Official Website of the NFL
https://www.nfl.com/

Rules of the NFL Draft
https://operations.nfl.com/the-players/the-nfl-draft/the-rules-of-the-draft/

Jets Select QB Sam Darnold
https://www.youtube.com/watch?v=TNRVy1L5iIQ

Works Consulted

"10—Franki Darnold." http://www.gorhody.com/sports/w-volley/2014-15/bios/darnold_franki_dcr5?view=bio.

"All Access: Jets Make the Call to Sam Darnold—New York Jets," http://www.newyorkjets.com/video/all-access-jets-make-the-call-to-sam-darnold-20590118.

Cimini, Rich. "Behind-the-scenes look at how Sam Darnold has impressed Jets." *ESPN*, 10 Aug. 2018. http://www.espn.com/blog/new-york-jets/post/_/id/76922/behind-the-scenes-look-at-how-sam-darnold-has-impressed-jets.

Dissecting Sam Darnold's preseason and his 'rare' QB traits." *ESPN*, 30 Aug. 2018. http://www.espn.com/blog/new-york/jets/post/_/id/77145/dissecting-sam-darnolds-preseason-and-his-rare-qb-traits.

Edwards, Josh. "Five Things to Know about USC QB Sam Darnold." 247Sports. https://247sports.com/nfl/cleveland-browns/Bolt/Things-to-know-about-NFLDraft-QB-Sam-Darnold-1172936386.

Hammond, Rich. "USC: Confident, patient Darnold has held his own in quarterback battle." *Orange County Register*. 15 April 2016. https://www.pe.com/2016/04/15/usc-confident-patient-darnold-has-held-his-own-in-quarterback-battle/.

Jenkins, Lee, "Trojan Force." *Sports Illustrated*. 14 August 2017, Vol. 127 Issue 5, p. 78-84.

Jones, Mike. "Palmer, Leinart high on Darnold. *USA Today*, 23 Apr. 2018, Sports Section, p. 1C.

"Meet Sam Darnold, the freshman quarterback who saved USC." *Foxsports*. 15 Nov. 2016. https://www.foxsports.com/college-football/story/usc-trojans-sam-darnold-washington-huskies-week-11-sports-illustrated-111016?amp=true.

McCollough, J. Brady. "Jets rookie quarterback Sam Darnold prepares for life on—and off—the field." *Los Angeles* Times, 23 July 2018. http://www.latimes.com/sports/usc/la-sp-sam-darnold-jets-20180723-story.html.

Pearlman, Jeff. "Sam Darnold Is the Realest." *B/R Magazine*. 27 August 2017. https://bleacherreport.com/articles/2725101-sam-darnold-usc-quaraaterback-childhood.

"Sam Darnold." https://www.sports-reference.com/cfb/players/sam-darnold-1.html.

"Sam Darnold Is Gone." *ESPN*, 4 Sept. 2017. p. 46-52.

"Sam Darnold Interview as Jets' QB" 2018 NFL Draft Apr—YouTube.

Schonbrun, Jeff. "New-Age Sam Darnold Tries to Solve an Age-Old Jets Problem." *New York Times*, 10 Sept. 2018. https://www.nytimes.com/2018/09/10/sports/football/sam-darnold-jets.html.

Uggetti, Paolo. "How Basketball Helped USC's Sam Darnold Become College Football's QB of the Moment." *The Ringer*. 31 Aug. 2017. https://www.theringer.com/2017/8/31/16230912/sam-darnold-usc-trojans-basketball-background.

Vasquez, Andy. "Sam Darnold: Anything less than Jets Super Bowl win is a failure." Northjersey.com.27 April 2018. http://www.northjersey.comstory/sports/nfl/jets/2018/04/27/sam-darnold-anything-less-than-new-york-ny-jets-super-bowl-win-failure-nfl-Draft-2018/5599.

Index

About the Author

Marylou Morano Kjelle is a college English professor and freelance writer who lives and works in Central New Jersey. Marylou has written nearly 60 nonfiction books for young people of all ages. Her sports biographies include Derrick Rose, Tim Howard, Josh Wolfe, and Alex Rodriquez. Marylou enjoyed writing about Sam Darnold, who plays for one of the two New Jersey "home football teams." She also learned a lot about football by researching and writing this book.

HAUNTED CASTLES AND FORTS

VIC KOVACS

CRABTREE
PUBLISHING COMPANY
WWW.CRABTREEBOOKS.COM

HAUNTED OR HOAX?

Author: Vic Kovacs

Editors: Marcia Abramson, Petrice Custance

Photo research: Melissa McClellan

Cover/interior design: T.J. Choleva

Proofreader: Lorna Notsch

**Production coordinator and
prepress technician:** Tammy McGarr

Print coordinator: Katherine Berti

Consultant: Susan Demeter-St. Clair
Paranormal Studies & Inquiry

Written and produced for Crabtree Publishing by
BlueAppleWorks Inc.

Photographs & Illustrations
Cover illustration: T.J Choleva (background image Melkor3D/Shutterstock; front image:
Szymon Kaczmarczyk/Shutterstock); Title page illustration: Joshua Avramson (background
image Melkor3D/Shutterstock; front image: e71lena/Shutterstock)
Shutterstock.com: © Login (page backgrounds); © Melkor3D (p. 4 right); © Carlos Caetano
(p. 5 bottom); © Andrey_Kuzmin (p. 5, 11 middle); © Imagine Photographer (p. 5, 9, 11, 15, 19,
21, 27, 29 sidebar); © Jiri Stoklaska (p. 6 top right); © e71lena (p. 4, 6 bottom, 11 middle bottom,
12 top); © Joseph Becker (p. 7, 19, 27 middle); © Ranta Images (p. 7 bottom right); hecke61 (p.
8 top right); © Kachalkina Veronika (p. 8 right); © Borisb17 (p. 9 top right); © Ensuper (p. 9,
21, 29 middle); Oldrich/Shutterstock.com (p. 10 top right); © Craig Duncanson (p. 10 bottom);
© Cristian Balate (p. 11 bottom right); © Vladimir Mulder (p. 9 sidebar); © Dontsu (p. 14 top
right); © yingko (p. 15 middle); © SusaZoom (p. 16–17 bottom); © Philip Bird LRPS CPAGB/
Shutterstock.com (p. 17 bottom right); © TaTum2003 (p. 17 sidebar); © Deyan Denchev (p. 19
top right); MilanMarkovic78 (p. 21 bottom right); © SF photo (p. 22 top right, 23 bottom left);
© Peyker (p. 23 middle); © lukaszsokol (p. 23 sidebar); © Claire McAdams (p. 23 bottom); ©
Darryl Brooks (p. 25 bottom); © Kletr (p. 25 sidebar); © NeonLight/Shutterstock.com (p. 26 top
right); © William Silver (p. 27 bottom); © Jan Kvita (p. 28 left); © Twinsterphoto (p. 28 middle);
© Fer Gregory (p. 28 right); © Korobach Evgeny (p. 28 bottom)
Creative Commons: iLongLoveKing (p. 11); Michael1010 (p. 14 bottom); Tony Hisgett (p. 15
top right); Rakami Art Studio (p. 18 top right); Parth.rkt (p. 18–19 bottom); Himanshu Yogi
(p. 19 left); Arpita Roy08 (p. 19 middle); JustSomePics (p. 23 top left); DrStew82 (p. 25 top)
Public Domain: National Portrait Gallery (p. 16 top right); Robert Jenkins Onderdonk (p. 26
bottom); Sir James Jebusa Shannon (p. 29 right)
Joshua Avramson (background Valery Sidelnykov/Shutterstock), p. 7, p. 8, p. 9 bottom right,
p. 13, p. 24 (background image Triple Tri/Creative Commons
Carlyn Iverson p. 12 bottom (background image Evdoha_spb/Shutterstock), p. 20, p. 22

Library and Archives Canada Cataloguing in Publication

Kovacs, Vic, author
Haunted castles and forts / Vic Kovacs.

(Haunted or hoax?)
Includes index.
Issued in print and electronic formats.
ISBN 978-0-7787-4629-4 (hardcover).--
ISBN 978-0-7787-4640-9 (softcover).--
ISBN 978-1-4271-2053-3 (HTML)

1. Haunted castles--Juvenile literature. 2. Fortification--Juvenile
literature. 3. Ghosts--Juvenile literature. I. Title.

BF1474.K68 2018   j133.1′22   C2017-907784-8
C2017-907785-6

Library of Congress Cataloging-in-Publication Data

CIP available at the Library of Congress

Crabtree Publishing Company
www.crabtreebooks.com   1-800-387-7650

Printed in the U.S.A./032018/BG20180202

Published in Canada
Crabtree Publishing
616 Welland Ave.
St. Catharines, Ontario
L2M 5V6

Published in the United States
Crabtree Publishing
PMB 59051
350 Fifth Avenue, 59th Floor
New York, New York 10118

Published in the United Kingdom
Crabtree Publishing
Maritime House
Basin Road North, Hove
BN41 1WR

Published in Australia
Crabtree Publishing
3 Charles Street
Coburg North
VIC, 3058

CONTENTS

MYTHS, GHOSTS, AND GHASTLY APPARITIONS

Most cultures have stories about the **afterlife**. In some it's a paradise, in others a nightmare. Sometimes it's a mix of both. But one kind of story has been told by almost every culture on Earth. It's the ghost story.

Ghostly Forms

Different ghost stories have been told for different reasons. Some are fiction, meaning they were completely made up. These are meant to entertain. Some ghost stories, though, are believed by some to be true. They're based on things that people really saw, or believe they did. Ghosts in these stories can take on a variety of forms. In some tales, they're apparitions. These are ghosts in the shape of a person or an animal, but without substance. Apparitions are often transparent, meaning you can see right through them. Other ghosts are an unseen force. They might move an object, blow a drape, or turn a light on and off. Sometimes, ghosts can be violent. These are known as **poltergeists**.

DID YOU KNOW?

Castles once served as the homes and fortresses of **nobles** and royalty. They were built on top of hills to keep enemies out. After cannons came along, walled **forts** were built. They had lower walls, with ditches and **ramparts** to absorb cannonball blasts. Nobles did not live in the forts, but soldiers did.

Gruesome History

Castles and forts are often thought to be haunted. This is because they are buildings with dramatic pasts. Often, these pasts were violent and bloody. It's believed that some ghosts of castles and forts are people who died in such terrible ways that they cannot pass on to the next life. Other ghosts may be people who died with unfinished business. They can't leave the site of their death without seeing their life's work completed. Whether or not you believe in ghosts, they're not the kind of places you'd like to spend the night.

For protection, castles only had tiny windows. This made the inside dark and gloomy—a perfect spot for ghosts!

PARANORMAL INVESTIGATIONS

The debate over the existence of ghosts goes on. There are many people on both sides. Those who don't believe in ghosts are called skeptics. Throughout the years, believers have used science and technology to try to prove that ghosts exist. Today, people who investigate the existence of ghosts are often called ghost hunters or **paranormal** investigators. If you've ever watched a TV show about ghost hunting, you've probably seen some of the gadgets they use. These include sound recorders, devices that can detect **electromagnetic** pulses, and cameras. Cameras are often equipped to record in night vision, or **infrared**. Skeptics believe that anything these devices spot or record can be easily explained by natural events. Ghost hunters are sure their devices show evidence of ghosts. Although there is no scientific proof at this time that ghosts exist, there is also no proof that they do *not* exist.

HOUSKA CASTLE— A GATEWAY TO HELL

In the 1200s, a village just north of the city of Prague had a problem. It was located near a huge hole in the ground. But this wasn't just any hole. It was so deep that it was impossible to see the bottom. There were reports of strange and terrible things, such as a half man and half beast, that would emerge from the hole at night. According to legend, some of these beings had wings. They were said to snatch villagers and drag them into the hole. The villagers believed that the pit was a doorway to hell.

Houska Castle was built without fortifications to keep enemies out. Yet it still stands today in the Czech Republic. It is not located near any trade routes that need protecting. This would all seem to point to the castle being built to keep something in, rather than to keep others out.

Tales spread far and wide about the monsters. People became afraid to go out at night if they were nearby.

Locking Them In

It was decided that a castle would be built on top of the hole to try and contain the doorway and its **demons**.

The castle was completed in 1278. The hole may have been covered up, but its evil didn't stop seeping through to the surface. Today, people say you can hear something scratching underneath the floor, trying to get out. There have been sightings of a frog-bulldog-human creature wandering the grounds. Walking shadows have whispered tales of murder to guests, and bleeding ghosts have terrified caretakers. There is also another spooky connection to the castle. **Nazis** used it as a base during World War II.

PIT OF HORRORS

According to local folklore, before construction of the castle started, all local prisoners who had been condemned to die were marched to the edge of the pit. It was there that they were offered a fate that may have been even worse. If they allowed themselves to be lowered into the pit, and reported back on what they saw, they would be freed.

One man was chosen to go first. He was slowly lowered into the hole. His screams started almost immediately. He was hurriedly pulled to the surface, and his appearance terrified everyone there. He had aged 30 years in a matter of moments. His hair was snow white, and his once smooth face was now broken with wrinkles. The man went mad and died two days later. The exact cause of his death was never known.

LOOK AT THE EVIDENCE

Because Houska Castle is so old, it's impossible to know how legends about it got started. What do you think? Is there a factual basis to stories of demons emerging from a doorway to hell? Or are the legends closer to a game of broken Telephone, in that they've been told so many times over hundreds of years that they've become exaggerated? Is it possible that the original stories were completely different from the versions told today?

THE WITCHES' CASTLE

Hundreds of years ago, a craze swept Europe and even spread to the Americas. During the 1600s, hundreds of people were accused of **witchcraft**. The accused often didn't have any way to defend themselves. They were often tortured into confessing to things they had never done. Once they admitted to these false actions, they were usually **executed**.

One place famous for its witch trials is Moosham Castle in Salzburg, Austria. Between 1675 and 1690, more than 100 people were brought there, accused of witchcraft. This is how it got its nickname of the Witches' Castle.

Moosham's spooky history didn't end with witch trials. In the 1800s, accused werewolves were tried there.

The suspected witches were held captive in the castle and tortured in the dungeons until they confessed.

Witch Trials

Unlike most places that held witch trials, the majority of the accused were male, and many were children and teenagers. Although it's impossible to know why all of them were accused, what is known is that almost all were poor **beggars**. Try to imagine being rounded up off the street and taken to a castle. There, you're accused of things you never did. The only people who can speak up for you are accused of the same crimes. It's under circumstances like this that more than 100 people were put to death. It's not surprising that some of them might come back, still unhappy with their fate.

Today, visitors to the castle report being touched and breathed on by unseen people. Sounds of banging and footsteps have also been heard, along with sightings of a mysterious white mist.

THE DOG MAIDEN OF SCHALLABURG CASTLE

Moosham Castle isn't the only haunted castle in Austria. Schallaburg Castle is said to be home to many ghosts who were unfairly condemned to die there. The voices of these ghosts are sometimes heard. However, the most famous resident is known as the Hunderfräulein, or Dog Maiden. It's said that a little girl with the head of a dog was born in the castle. She was considered a monster and kept in the cellars. Now she roams there, often appearing before a tragic event.

LOOK AT THE EVIDENCE

If there was ever a place that was likely to really be haunted, it's Moosham Castle, due to all the pain, suffering, and death the castle has seen. While we might never know if the castle is really haunted, we do know it's extremely unlikely any of the people executed there were actually witches. In almost every witchhunt throughout history, there was an ulterior motive. That means people usually had a secret reason for accusing someone of being a witch. Sometimes, it was to try to get the accused's property. Other times, it was an attempt to wipe out a disliked group. That seems to be the case at Moosham, where most of the accused witches were beggars. It may have been unacceptable to kill someone for begging, but it was fine to kill beggars who were labeled witches.

THE ALNWICK CASTLE VAMPIRE

Alnwick Castle, in Northumberland, England, has stood for almost 1,000 years. In that time, it has become home to the Percy family, the head of which holds the title of Duke of Northumberland. The family was once known as the "Kings in the North" for their rebellion against the English king. It is the second-largest inhabited castle in the country, after Windsor Castle. In the 1200s, it may have been home to quite a spooky resident.

Harry Potter and the Sorcerer's Stone *was filmed at Alnwick. Movie magic turned it into Hogwarts.*

Some of Alnwick, including the cellars and a poison garden, are open for tours in the summer.

Hunchbacked Vampire

It is said that in the 1200s, a man from Yorkshire was known for his crimes and low **morals**. He fled to Alnwick Castle, where he had friends. There, he did well and was eventually named a lord. He even managed to find a wife!

One day, the man had a terrible fall. A priest was called, but for some reason, the man refused to confess his sins. He soon died from his injuries. However, he may have not stayed in his grave for long. Reports of a terrifying, hunchbacked vampire soon spread through nearby villages. The vampire was said to drain his victims of their blood. It was also claimed that he spread disease and sickness wherever he went.

BRAN CASTLE, ROMANIA

Bran Castle is a beautiful landmark in Romania with a dark side. It likely inspired the count's castle in Bram Stoker's novel *Dracula*. The castle was linked to a cruel ruler, Vlad Tepes, in the 1500s. He was known as Vlad Dracul and Vlad the Impaler. Some say his ghost roams Bran Castle. Certainly, his name lives on!

Many ideas about vampires come from the 1897 novel, although vampire tales had been told worldwide for centuries. Today, vampires are said to be undead, neither truly alive nor truly dead. They feed on the blood of the living. They hate sunlight, garlic, and crosses. Can you think of other vampire "facts"?

Bran Castle still attracts visitors hoping to glimpse Dracula.

Good Riddance

Eventually, the villagers had enough. A local priest gathered a large group that went to the former lord's grave. After digging up his body, they pierced his heart. It's said fresh blood poured from the wound. The villagers believed this was proof that he was a vampire. They cut off the lord's head and burned the body, hoping they had rid themselves of the curse.

According to legend, the priest and villagers destroyed the body of the Alnwick vampire but not its evil spirit. The vampire's angry ghost haunts the castle, causing strange events and misfortunes.

PLAGUE YEARS

Plague swept through Europe in the mid-1300s. Nearly a third of the population died from what came to be known as the Black Death. Fleas on rats spread the disease, but that wasn't known at the time. People blamed witches, vampires, or anyone who seemed different. They tried to ward off plague with magic and spells, but outbreaks continued for centuries.

12

Ghost of the Grey Lady

The vampire lord wasn't the only **supernatural** being to call Alnwick Castle home. There's also the story of the Grey Lady. She's believed to be a maid who worked at the castle many years ago. Apparently, while performing her duties in the kitchen, she fell down a **chute** into tunnels underneath the castle. The chute housed a dumbwaiter, a kind of small elevator used to move food from one floor to another. Luckily for her, the fall didn't kill her. Unluckily, the dumbwaiter chose that exact moment to break. It fell directly on top of her. She was immediately crushed to death. People still claim to see her ghost, wandering the tunnels beneath the castle.

Maybe the Grey Lady's ghost is still searching for the chute she was killed in, hoping to finally find her way out!

LOOK AT THE EVIDENCE

*Many cultures have their own ghost tales, witch stories, and vampire legends. Most of these tales are very old. They may have started as a way to explain misfortunes that areas were going through. For example, many people today believe the Alnwick Castle vampire may have been invented to explain the spread of the plague in the villages around the castle. There are also some medical conditions that may have led to certain people being called vampires. **Albinism** is a condition that causes some people to lack **pigment** in their skin. This makes them appear pale, and can give them a sensitivity to sunlight. Sound familiar?*

HAUNTED LEAP CASTLE

Leap Castle in Ireland has had an incredibly bloody history. Built by the O'Bannon clan, the castle may have claimed its first victim before it was even built. The legend goes that two O'Bannon brothers were fighting for leadership of the family. They decided that a contest of strength would settle it. They both agreed to jump from a high rock on the site of the future castle. Whoever survived would become leader. The legend doesn't say which brother, if either, survived. This deadly leap is apparently where the castle gets its name.

No one is quite sure when Leap Castle in Ireland was built. Different reports place the date from the 1100s to as late as the 1400s.

DID YOU KNOW?

Ireland is famous for tales of fairies, spirits, and ghosts of all kinds. One of the most famous is the banshee. This female spirit often takes the form of an old **crone**. The banshee is known for its horrible moaning. If you hear these cries, watch out! It's said they're a warning of death.

According to folklore, banshees often have long, flowing hair that is silver or white. Most have red eyes from weeping, though at least one legend tells of a headless banshee who carries a bowl of blood.

O'Carroll Clan Takes Over

Leap Castle was quickly taken over by the brutal O'Carroll clan. Their time there was marked by a number of horrors. One of the most famous was another battle over leadership between brothers. After the head of the O'Carrolls died, there was no clear choice to take over for him. His sons, Thaddeus and Teighe, both claimed the leadership. One day, Teighe, a priest, was leading mass in the castle's chapel. Suddenly, Thaddeus burst in and murdered him on the spot. Since then, that room has been known as the Bloody Chapel.

Captain Darby's Treasure

Teighe's ghost isn't the only one said to haunt Leap Castle. There's also the Wild Captain. Captain Darby had been a prisoner in the castle, but eventually he and an O'Carroll daughter fell in love. After marrying, he became head of the castle. Later, he was jailed in Dublin for treason. His years in jail drove him nearly mad. When he got home, he could not remember where he had hidden his treasure in the walls. It's said his ghost is still searching today.

The Croft family sold the castle in 1746, but bought it back in 1923. It is now part of the National Trust, which preserves British history.

CROFT CASTLE, ENGLAND

Croft Castle is said to be one of the most haunted places in England. Parts of this huge house were built in the 1400s. Since then, it has become home to at least seven different ghosts. The most famous of these is a huge man in a sleeveless leather jacket. He's thought to be Owain Glyndwr, a member of the Croft family by marriage. In life, Glyndwr fought for Welsh freedom. In death, he's still apparently a very imposing figure!

WHITE LADY OF CORFE CASTLE

Corfe Castle was first built by William the Conquerer, the first Norman king of England. It was built not long after the Norman Conquest of the country, around 1066. At the time, most castles in England were built out of earth and wood. Corfe, however, was much tougher, being one of the first castles built with stone. Built on top of a hill, the impressive castle commanded a good view of the surrounding area.

After standing for almost one thousand years, it's not surprising that some people have met with a gruesome end at Corfe Castle. People have heard an unseen child sobbing in a nearby cabin. They've also heard an entire Roman army marching down the hillsides around the castle. But the most famous ghost at Corfe Castle is the White Lady.

DID YOU KNOW?

William the Conqueror built a network of castles to help his Norman forces control England. His men came to England from Normandy, which is just across the English Channel. It is now part of France.

Both the Celts and the Romans had strongholds at the site of Corfe Castle, but only ruins remain there now.

Headless Ghost

Nobody knows exactly who she was in life. The most well-known story says she was at the castle during the English Civil War. This was a war between Royalists, who were loyal to the English king, and those who wanted to get rid of the **monarchy**. Corfe Castle was one of the last Royalist holdouts in the area. It's said that a young girl betrayed the castle to enemy troops, which led to its destruction. Now, her headless, shimmering ghost is cursed to wander its grounds, terrifying all those she encounters.

LOOK AT THE EVIDENCE

The White Lady is Corfe Castle's most famous ghost. However, she isn't the only spirit to go by that name. A lady dressed all in white is one of the most commonly seen apparitions at supposedly haunted places. Dozens of white ladies have been reported all over the world! Does it seem at all odd that sightings of women in white clothing are so common? Can you think of any reasons people see the same thing in so many different places, so far apart? What do you think?

DUNSTER CASTLE, ENGLAND

Dunster Castle, in Somerset, England, shares many similarities with Corfe Castle. Like Corfe, it was built on top of a hill. The two castles were also first built at about the same time. And also like Corfe, it is apparently very haunted. People who work in the castle have reported a number of eerie events. A severed human foot suddenly appeared in front of a person in the kitchen one day. Others have heard voices in empty rooms. There is also one spot on the property everyone knows to avoid—the dungeon.

A seven-foot-tall skeleton was found in the dungeon, chained by the wrists and ankles. He was found with the skeletal remains of several other prisoners. The bones were found in a section that is permanently dark, letting in no sunshine. The dungeon produces such a feeling of dread that some people refuse to go anywhere near it.

BHANGARH FORT— LOCKED AFTER DUSK

Bhangarh Fort is located in Rajasthan province in India. It is believed to be the most haunted place in the country. The area around it has become a ghost town, also named Bhangarh, because no one wants to live nearby. The ruins are so eerie, it's easy to see why.

According to legend, Bhangarh was once a busy area with temples, a marketplace, and even a royal palace. Then it came under a curse and fell into ruin, possibly all in one day. But what caused the fort's ruin, and why has it remained so cursed? Locals tell two different stories to explain its misfortune.

Bhangarh was built in 1573. There is no exact date, though, for when it became a ruin.

Once people leave for the day, animals from the nearby forest take shelter in the fort. This may account for some of the strange noises and rustling heard at night.

Deadly Shadow

In the first story, it is said that a holy man named Bulu Nath lived and **meditated** in the area where the fort was to be built. The emperor Mando Singh got Bulu Nath's permission to construct the fort, but on one condition. No building's shadow could fall on the holy man's home. However, once it was finished, the emperor's palace was too tall. When its shadow touched Bulu Nath's house, he cursed the entire city, dooming it.

By day, the ancient palaces and temples seem serene and peaceful.

LARNACH CASTLE, NEW ZEALAND

William Lanarch was a successful businessman and politician. He started building himself a castle in 1871 in the city of Dunedin. It took four years.

Almost as soon as he moved in, Larnach began suffering a series of tragedies. In a fairly short amount of time, his daughter and his first and second wives passed away. Today, the castle is a beautiful tourist destination. However, some guests have reported ghostly occurrences. People have been pushed, shelves have been seen shaking, and people have even claimed to have difficulty breathing in certain rooms. Is it possible that the tragedies of over a hundred years ago are still echoing through the castle?

Beauty and Black Magic

The second story tells of a wizard and a princess. Ratnavati was said to be the most beautiful and graceful maiden in all the land. As soon as she turned 18, princes and other gentlemen from all over proposed to her. But there was also a powerful magician who had fallen in love with her. Knowing he was not noble enough for her, he decided to use his black magic to win her heart. When the princess went shopping for scented oil, the wizard used his powers to turn it into a very strong love potion. However, the princess realized what he had done. She tossed the oil onto the ground. There, it turned into a giant boulder and rolled toward the wizard, crushing him. With his dying breath, he cursed Bhangarh and all in it. Not long after, the city was destroyed by an enemy army from the north. Everyone there was slaughtered, including the princess.

Locals say the spirits of the wizard and Ratnavati still roam the ruins. The princess is expected to return someday in a new form to end the curse.

Overcautious Government?

While these stories might just be legends, they're taken seriously. The belief that the ruined fort is dangerously haunted has become widespread. It's illegal to enter it after dark. Trespassers face heavy punishments if they're found. The Archaeological Survey of India has even posted a sign warning people not to enter past sunset. Why are the authorities so strict? It's said that in the past people who entered after dark were never seen again. People have also heard screams and other chilling sounds and have smelled strange perfumes from inside the fort. Regardless of what you think of the legends, the government certainly seems to think there's something off about Bhangarh Fort. That should probably be warning enough.

TERRIFIED TOURISTS

Many tourists visit Bhangarh. Over the years, they have added stories to the legend. One story says that a bus carrying students home after a trip to the fort crashed mysteriously. Another tells of a group of tourists who broke the law and went into the fort at night. They bribed a gatekeeper to let them in. He told them the fort was haunted but took their money anyway. The tourists were having fun, until they came upon a boy in a room that had no doors, only a tiny window covered by a grill. No one could get in or out—except a ghost.

LOOK AT THE EVIDENCE

The government's refusal to allow anyone into Bhangarh Fort past dark certainly points to there being something there. Could there be another explanation, though? The fort is a popular tourist attraction in the daytime. For a certain group of people, it only becomes more appealing if there's an air of danger to it. After all, haven't you ever wanted to do something just because it's forbidden? Ghost tourism is also a very popular industry. People who are interested in the supernatural will flock to a place if they think there's a chance of seeing something out of the ordinary. What do you think? Is Bhangarh Fort really haunted? Or is it just a case of hype?

HAUNTED FORTS IN NORTH AMERICA

North America doesn't have any castles as ancient as those found in Europe and the rest of the world. Yet it still has plenty of haunted buildings. It has been the site of a number of bloody and terrible battles and wars. As a result, North America has many haunted forts.

Fort Niagara is near Youngstown, New York, on Lake Ontario.

Fort Niagara, New York

During the almost 300 years it has stood, Fort Niagara has been home to French, British, and American troops. Its most notorious ghost, however, isn't the victim of war or battle. It's said that while the French still held the fort, two soldiers had a **duel** over a woman. One of the soldiers gained the upper hand and killed his comrade. He quickly realized that he could be hanged for his crime and tried to hide the evidence. So, he cut off his opponent's head and flung it into Lake Ontario. He then dumped the body down a well. It's said that on certain nights, the murdered soldier's ghost rises out of the well and searches the fort for his lost head.

Fort Henry, Ontario, Canada

Fort Henry is often considered the most haunted place in Canada. The fort was built in Kingston during the War of 1812. It was later expanded and reinforced in the 1830s. Although it was never attacked, it held a number of prisoners over the years. Executions were common. Visitors have reported seeing a number of apparitions, including one man wearing a blue military uniform. This is thought to be Nils Von Schoultz, who was hanged for his role in a failed rebellion against British rule in 1837.

During the day, a group called the Fort Henry Guard reenacts life at the fort for visitors. At night, ghost tours are offered.

GHOSTS OF 1812

In 1812, the young nation of the United States went to war with mighty Britain again. The two countries had many disagreements even after the American Revolution. Americans did not believe that Britain respected their new nation and its independence. The British feared that the Americans would try to take over Canada while Britain was busy fighting against Emperor Napoleon of France.

The U.S. and Britain fought fiercely on land, at sea, and on the Great Lakes. The British even burned Washington, D.C., in 1814. More than 20,000 soldiers and sailors had died in battle or from disease by the time the fighting ended in 1815. The U.S. kept its independence. But little was changed by the deaths of so many. Their ghosts are said to haunt battle sites and forts.

Fort Meigs, Toledo, Ohio

Like many forts in North America, Fort Meigs was first established for the War of 1812. It was founded by William Henry Harrison, the future president. Although it was only in operation for about a year, it was put under siege twice and saw its fair share of action. Visitors to the site today have heard sounds of war such as cannons and muskets firing and flutes and drums playing. They've also heard marching, with none of these sounds having any clear explanation. Some believe they're the sounds of the 500 British, Canadian, and **Indigenous** soldiers thought to be buried under and around the fort.

Like many old forts, Fort Meigs hosts a ghost walk in October to raise funds for preservation. Visitors encounter "apparitions" but it's all in Halloween fun!

Fort Adams, Newport, Rhode Island

Fort Adams was completed in 1799, and was in service, in one form or another, until 1854. Local soldiers called militiamen were stationed there during the War of 1812. Many of the ghosts who are thought to haunt it weren't killed by enemy soldiers. Some died from illnesses, some from accidents. Others were murdered by their fellow soldiers in disagreements. One story tells of a soldier who got angry with his friend and threw rocks at him. His friend turned around and shot him dead. This might be why the ghosts at Fort Adams have such an angry reputation. They're known for poking, shoving, and, yes, even throwing rocks.

Fort Adams was built to protect the coast and shipping lanes. Today, it is part of a state historical park.

FORT KNOX, MAINE

The United States has two famous forts named Fort Knox. The one in Kentucky is famous for holding much of the nation's gold. The one in Maine is famous for paranormal activity. It is considered one of the most haunted places in the country. The TV show *Ghost Hunters* visited the fort, and there are books and websites about it. Visitors report seeing apparitions, hearing voices, and feeling spirits touching them. Yet Fort Knox has never been involved in a battle. Some locals say spirits always roamed the area, according to the Indigenous peoples who first lived there.

The fort's most famous apparition is Sergeant Leopold Hegyi, who was caretaker from 1887 to 1900. He was alone for most of that time. Many think his lonely ghost still roams the fort, doing his job. A tour guide has reported catching an image that looked like Hegyi with her camera.

Another visitor said his camera showed the image of a girl with a bonnet, a caped figure, and a little boy. Visitors today can tell of their encounters on the fort's website. Read them and make up your own mind!

The Alamo

The Alamo, in San Antonio, Texas, is the site of one of history's most famous battles. Even people who are not sure what happened there probably have heard the rallying cry "Remember the Alamo!"

Thirteen days of historical events are held each year to mark the anniversary of the Alamo siege.

Fearsome Battle

Texas was fighting for independence from Mexico in 1835. In December, Texas soldiers and volunteers took over a fort called the Alamo. Mexico sent thousands of soldiers to get it back. For 13 days, they bombarded the former mission church. On March 6, Mexican forces stormed the weakened Alamo. The defenders fought fiercely, but the Mexicans massacred them all. Only a few women and children survived to tell the tale.

According to legend, Davy Crockett ran out of bullets and used his rifle as a club at the Alamo. That's the image in this painting from 1903, but historians say it may be a myth.

The Magnificent Six

The famous Texas fort is home to a number of ghost stories and eerie legends. Many people have claimed to see ghosts coming out of the walls, as well as hearing screams and explosions. However, the most striking ghostly event happened not long after the original battle. According to the legend, Mexican troops were ordered to destroy the Alamo. Upon their arrival, however, they were met by six apparitions waving ghostly swords. "Do not touch the Alamo!" they shouted. "Do not touch these walls!" The Mexican troops did not achieve their goal, and the Alamo still stands today.

GHOST OF DAVY CROCKETT

Davy Crockett was a legendary American frontiersman who became even more famous in the 1950s, thanks to a popular Disney TV show. Kids all over America dressed like Davy. The theme song proclaimed him "King of the Wild Frontier." He deserved the title, as he was an explorer, a hunter, and even a congressman from Tennessee. After he died, people didn't want to believe it. They said they saw him—alive—all over the country. Then people started seeing his ghost. Park rangers at the Alamo say he is one of many spirits there. He still stands guard, holding his **flintlock** rifle.

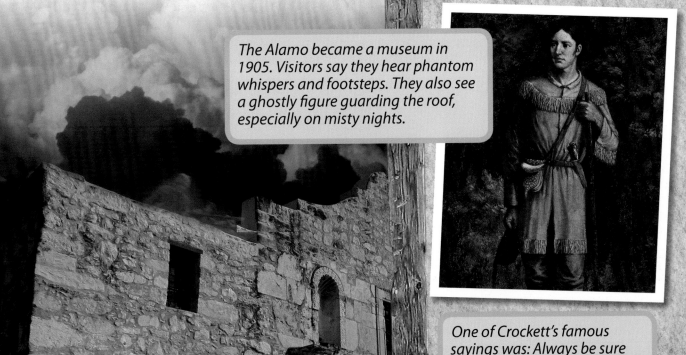

The Alamo became a museum in 1905. Visitors say they hear phantom whispers and footsteps. They also see a ghostly figure guarding the roof, especially on misty nights.

One of Crockett's famous sayings was: Always be sure you are right, then go ahead.

WHAT DO YOU THINK?

People have claimed to have seen ghosts for pretty much all of human history. Even today, there are encounters that science has a very hard time explaining. However, much of the time there's another reason for saying a place might be haunted. Just think about all the people who love to be scared, who would love to see a real ghost. They would probably pay money for the chance to see one. Ghost tourism is a huge industry that has helped a lot of people and places financially.

So the next time someone tells you they saw a ghost, or heard phantom footsteps, take a moment. Is there another reason they might be telling you about it?

Many people bring their cameras on ghost tours. But no one has been able to prove the existence of ghosts with a photo.

People Love to Get Scared!

People tell ghost stories for a number of reasons. Some of them are cautionary tales, warning people today about dangers that still exist in the world. Some are a way to keep history alive and make it fun for new generations. And some are just scary. After all, people love to get scared! It's why there are so many horror movies and books and video games. It can be fun, especially when you know deep down that you're safe. Maybe some of those stories even have a basis in fact.

FAMOUS HOAXES

HARRY HOUDINI – THE MEDIUM BUSTER

Harry Houdini, an American, was one of the most famous and talented magicians of all time. He lived from 1874 to 1926, a time when seances were wildly popular. Houdini was a believer in ghosts at first. However, he became very doubtful once he noticed that many mediums were using stage magicians' tricks for fake seances. Houdini thought that was a disgrace and wanted people to know the truth. He became a medium buster. He would go to a seance in disguise, then tear it off as he jumped up to show how the trick was being done. People flocked to his stage shows to watch him re-create both the seance and the dramatic reveal at the end.

THE ORIGINAL GHOSTBUSTER

It's only natural for people to want to communicate with loved ones they have lost. This is especially true after disasters and wars. After the Civil War, for example, many Americans held seances and consulted mediums. A seance is a gathering of people trying to talk to the dead. Mediums are people who say they can do so. Seances and mediums became extremely popular in the 1800s in Europe and America.

While some people believed in the mediums, others suspected that they were frauds trying to make money and become famous. An English scientist and teacher, Eleanor Sidgwick, is often called the first ghostbuster. She headed a group called the Society for Psychical Research. She exposed some fake mediums and cast doubt on the whole practice of seances. The Society for Psychical Research is still around today, carrying out research of paranormal phenomena.

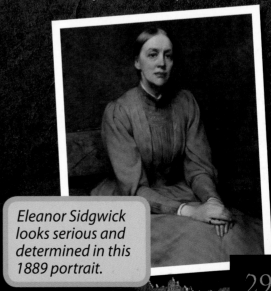

Eleanor Sidgwick looks serious and determined in this 1889 portrait.

BOOKS

Castle: Revised and in Full Color by David Macaulay. HMH Books for Young Readers, 2013.

Everything Castles by Crispin Boyer. National Geographic Children's Books, 2011.

Haunted! Edinburgh Castle by Ryan Nagelhout. Gareth Stevens, 2013.

Haunted Histories: Creepy Castles, Dark Dungeons, and Powerful Palaces by J. H. Everett and Marilyn Scott-Waters. Square Fish, 2013.

Haunted! The Tower of London by Drew Nelson. Gareth Stevens, 2013.

WEBSITES

The Alamo

www.history.com/topics/alamo

The 10 Most Haunted Castles in Europe

www.thecrazytourist.com/the-10-most-haunted-castles-in-europe/

History of Castles

www.primaryhomeworkhelp.co.uk/Castles.html

The 10 Most Haunted Forts in the United States

www.urbanghostsmedia.com/2013/08/10-most-haunted-forts-in-the-united-states/

Fort Knox, Maine

http://fortknox.maineguide.com/Hauntnews.html

The Society for Psychical Research

www.spr.ac.uk/

GLOSSARY

afterlife The place some people believe we go when we die

albinism A condition from birth in which a person lacks pigment in their skin, hair, and eyes

beggar A very poor person who must ask others for help

chute An open or enclosed passage way that is sloped

crone An old woman who is ugly and may be cruel

demon A kind of evil spirit said to live in hell

duel A planned fight with weapons between two people

electromagnetic An interaction of electric and magnetic fields

executed Put to death

flintlock An old type of gun in which a piece of flint was used to light the gunpowder

fort Usually a type of military encampment known for being surrounded by strong walls

Indigenous The first people to live in a place

infrared Light that is outside of the visible spectrum

meditate Think deeply

monarchy A government whose head is a member of royalty

morals Beliefs about choosing between right and wrong

Nazis The group that controlled Germany from 1933 to 1945 and committed many atrocities

noble A person born to a socially high-ranked family

paranormal Unable to be explained by science

pigment A coloring substance in the tissue of people, animals, and plants

plague A disease that spreads easily from person to person and kills most of the people who get it

poltergeist A troublesome spirit

ramparts Protective barriers, often made of dirt or debris or both

supernatural Having to do with the spirit world rather than the physical word

witchcraft The use of magic

INDEX